For Wendi G,
and all the trees

𝒜
atheneum

ATHENEUM BOOKS FOR YOUNG READERS

An imprint of Simon & Schuster Children's Publishing Division

1230 Avenue of the Americas, New York, New York 10020

© 2022 by Toni Yuly

Book design by Rebecca Syracuse © 2022 by Simon & Schuster, Inc.

All rights reserved, including the right of reproduction in whole or in part in any form.

ATHENEUM BOOKS FOR YOUNG READERS is a registered trademark of

Simon & Schuster, Inc. Atheneum logo is a trademark of Simon & Schuster, Inc.

For information about special discounts for bulk purchases, please

contact Simon & Schuster Special Sales at 1-866-506-1949

or business@simonandschuster.com.

The Simon & Schuster Speakers Bureau can bring authors to your live event.

For more information or to book an event, contact the Simon & Schuster

Speakers Bureau at 1-866-248-3049 or visit our website at www.simonspeakers.com.

The text for this book was set in Maku.

The illustrations for this book were rendered in chalk pastel, torn tissue paper,

cut paper, pen and ink, pencil, and digital collage.

Manufactured in China

1221 SCP

First Edition

10 9 8 7 6 5 4 3 2 1

Library of Congress Cataloging-in-Publication Data

Names: Yuly, Toni, author, illustrator.

Title: Some questions about trees / Toni Yuly.

Description: First edition. | New York : Atheneum Books for Young Readers, [2022] | Audience: Ages 4 to 8. |

Summary: A curious child wonders if tiny trees dream of being big, if the tallest trees get lonely, and what part is the heart of a tree.

Identifiers: LCCN 2020052231 | ISBN 9781534489158 (hardcover) | ISBN 9781534489165 (ebook)

Subjects: CYAC: Trees—Fiction. | Questions and answers—Fiction.

Classification: LCC PZ7.Y89655 So 2022 | DDC [E]—dc23

LC record available at https://lccn.loc.gov/2020052231

Some Questions About Trees

TONI YULY

Atheneum Books for Young Readers

New York London Toronto Sydney New Delhi

Where do trees live?

On the earth . . .

or in the sky?

Are some trees shy?

Are some trees full of friends?

What part

is the heart

of a tree?

Is fall

when trees

throw parties

with leaves?

Is that why trees are

naked in winter?

Who tells the trees

when spring is here?

Who do fruit trees

make fruit for?

Do tiny trees dream
of being big?

Do the tallest trees get lonely?

Are trees afraid of the dark,

or does the moon keep them company?

Does my favorite tree . . .

remember me?

When I plant a tree . . .

are we family?